Christmas Eve! Santa was making his rounds with a sled full of toys.

To his surprise, The Ghost was flying all around him.

The reindeer were scare! Out of control. Jumping up and down, yelling. The toys were flying out of the sled and all over the clouds.

2

Santa panic! Call 911 in Orbit for help. A big ball of fire roll out from the clouds, made a dead stop in front of Santa.

It turned into a creature with long arms that came out of his ears. Radar fire eyes and a face like a pear. It barked like a Dog, wolf, wolf!

Fear not Santa, I am a ghost chaser. Wolf, wolf. He grabbed the ghost and threw them up into the sky and locked them up in his castle way down in the dungeon.

The ghost chaser got the toys back in the sled and help Santa get back on his way to deliver the toys.

The ghost chaser turn back into a ball of
fire and barked wolf, wolf and disappeared.
Santa was very nervous after this ordeal.

Whoops, he slipped down the chimney
head first with the bag of toys. Ho!Ho!Ho!
Done with his duties he went back up.

8

So after Santa left, the ghost went in and stole all the toys. They even eat the cookies and drank the milk.

The Children were very disappointed and started to cry.

The father out of desperation call Santa.
The little one have been so good. Santa
told him to call 911 in orbit. We are being
invaded by the Ghosts.

Don't be scare, I am a ghost chaser, like a ball of fire and a bark, wolf, wolf, I am re-turning the children's toys.

Santa's mansion in the North Pole. The
ghost are invading his home. Rose, one of
the servants and the elves were all scared.
They all hid in a closet.

The ghost chaser was on his way. He made a sudden stop at Santas and took care of the ghost with a quick bark. Wolf, wolf he said and they were gone.

13

Santa got on one knee and purposed to his long time friend, Rose. Be mine my love. She answered "yes, yes my heart is yours."

They were happy and kissed. Santa said Ho!Ho!Ho!

The special Valentines was here. Everyone gathered at the Church.

The wedding took place on that day. Santa and his new wife, Rose cut the cake. The elf's eat like there was no tomorrow.

Santa and Rose danced until dawn. The elfs had to clean up the place before they could turn in for the night.

Rose told Santa one day that she was pregnant. Santa was very happy. He could not wait for the great event to take place.

So the day arrived, and Santa call for an Ambulance to take Rose to the Hospital. Its time my dear, a kiss from Santa and away they went.

Santa was nervous, shaking.

He went to the waiting room.

He decided to stop off and get a cup of coffee since he had no idea how long this would take.

He was so nervous he started drinking cup after cup. He drank a lot of coffee.

Back to the waiting room. A nurse came out and announced "IT'S A GIRL!" but wait, the doctor steps in and said " wait, there is another girl…"

Santa, your now the proud father of three beautiful little girls. Santa fainted flat on the floor.

The ghost were on the roof waiting for everyone to be a sleep so they could steal the
babies.

The ghost saw there chance and swoop in. The baby girls started to cry so loud that everyone woke up.

Santa jumped into action and called 911 in
orbit the ghost chasers. In a flash he saved
all of his new baby girls.

The ghost chaser threw the ghost in the dungeon and lock the door. He even threw the keys away.

Santa was now safe and so was his family.
They all lived happily ever after.

Merry Christmas

And

God Bless us all.

Story was written and illustrated by:

Flossie Langdon Ward

About the author:

Flossie is 87 years old and was born in

Ontario, Canada in October of 1927.

Published in agreement with:

Createspace Inc.

Merry Christmas

God Bless

www.ingramcontent.com/pod-product-compliance
Lightning Source LLC
Chambersburg PA
CBHW041637050726

47507CB00026B/214